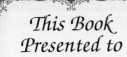

This Book
Presented to

Weaver

From

Summit County
Clean Communities

November 20, 1992

B311

View from the Air

CHARLES LINDBERGH'S EARTH AND SKY

By Reeve Lindbergh · Photographs by Richard Brown

Viking

INTRODUCTION

Throughout his life, my father, Charles Lindbergh, loved the earth and the sky. He came to know the earth as a boy growing up on a family farm in Little Falls, Minnesota, and he came to know the sky as one of America's pioneer aviators, best known for his famous nonstop solo flight from New York to Paris in 1927, in *The Spirit of St. Louis*.

Charles Lindbergh's career covered many fields of interest, from aviation to military research to biomedical studies to experimentation with the earliest ventures in rocketry and space exploration.

My father wrote about many of these things in his books, but in all of his writings, throughout the whole of his life, one theme appeared more often than any other: his great love and concern for the natural world. The longer he flew over the earth, the more convinced he became that we must protect it from the disruptions created as our society advanced, even though the advances might be as exciting as the airplanes he himself had helped to make famous.

Once, many years after his flight to Paris, he confessed, "If I had to choose, I would rather have birds than airplanes." He went on to say that if we humans truly learned to take care of our planet, we would never have to make such a choice.

During the 1960s, he wrote a number of articles warning us that we must learn to protect our earth, and to balance our commitment to expanding technology with care for the natural environment. He thought that people, in this increasingly complicated modern world, could still learn from nature, which he said "thrives on infinite complication. No problem has been too difficult for it to solve. From the dynamics of an atom, nature produces the tranquility of a flower, the joy of a porpoise, the intellect of man — the miracle of life." He wrote this in an article called "The Wisdom of Wildness." In the last sentences of that essay he said, "The human future depends upon our ability to combine the knowledge of science with the wisdom of wildness."

The last flights that Charles Lindbergh made as a pilot were over the landscape of rural New England during 1971 and 1972. He flew with a young friend, Richard Brown, a landscape and nature photographer who wondered what aerial photography might be like. Lindbergh offered to be Richard's pilot. They rented a plane at a small airport in Montpelier, and together the pilot and the photographer flew many times over the farms and forests and wilderness areas of northern New England. Almost all the photographs in *View from the Air* were taken during these flights.

I wrote the poem in memory of my father, of the things he said and the things he saw. He did not write or talk exactly as I do, but in this poem I am pretending a little. I am imagining that the speaker is an early pilot who, like Lindbergh, has been flying for a lifetime, and is talking to the rest of us about his perspective and feelings. He has something he wants to leave with us — the lifetime love of earth and sky that is every pilot's view from the air.

—R. L.

This was the course of the river,
And this was the lay of the land.
All through my life I flew over
Nature's best offer to man.

4

This was the world I discovered.

Each year, each season I'd fly,

Watching the earth like a lover,

This was my view from the sky.

One tree alone in a pasture,

One church alone on a hill,

One man alone in an airplane,

Sharing a morning quite still.

8

10

I saw the towns on the hillsides,

Winter-deep dreaming in snow:

Church steeples reaching to heaven,

Village homes nestled below.

12

I saw the farms in the valleys
Waking at first light of day.
I saw the sun touch the roof lines,
I watched the mist lift away.

I saw the hay fields and pastures
High-rolling under my wing:
Harvests of gold in the autumn,
Furrows plowed under in spring.

I saw the trees of the forest,
Transformed by distance and light,
Softer than gardens of feathers
From the perspective of flight.

I saw the wild lands and waters
Scattered with sunlight and rain.
Earth's oldest wisdom is wildness:
Wildness must always remain.

14

Earth was our generous mother.

Land, sea and sky, all were ours:

Forests and mountains and rivers,

Beasts, birds and fish, fruits and flowers.

When did the dust haze the prairies?

How did the smoke fill our skies?

19

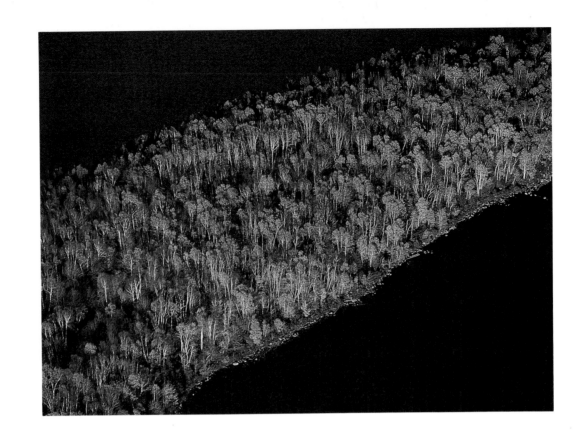

Who stained these lakes and these oceans?

When will we learn to be wise?

Earth can still heal and recover
Given our time and our care.
Some things have vanished forever,
But earth will remain, and repair.

22

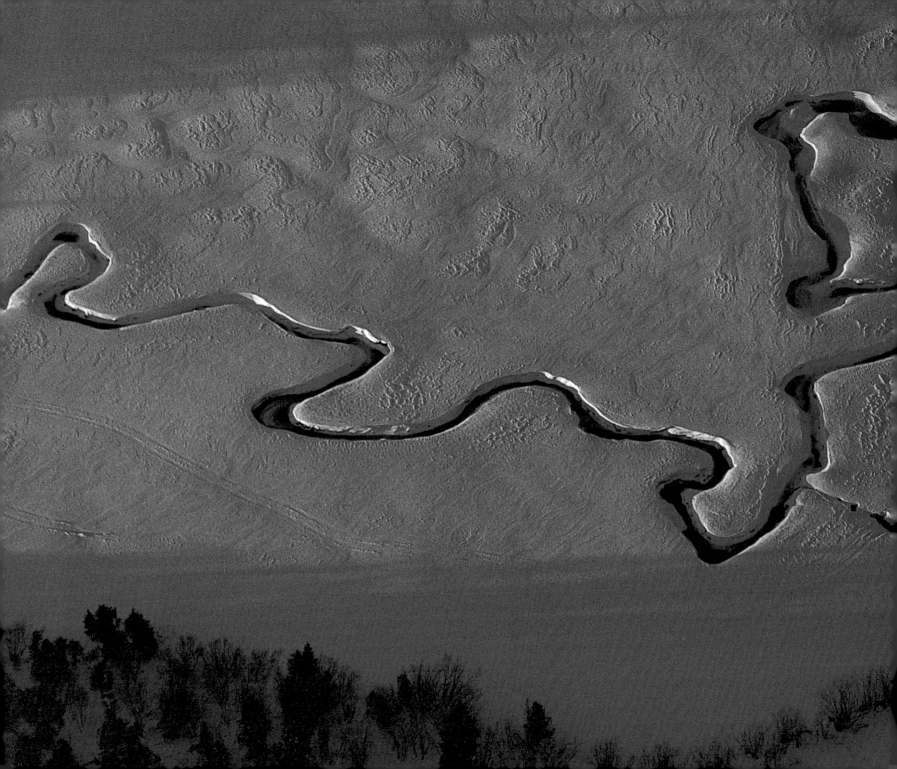

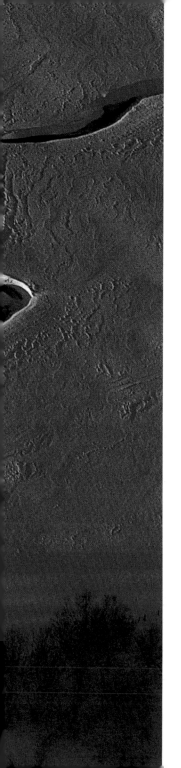

Flying above, how I loved it!

Learned to make this truth my own:

Nature's best loved at a distance;

What you would keep, leave alone.

25

I knew the whiteness of winter,

I knew the fires of the fall,

26

Warm springs, and sweet-scented summers,

I knew them, flew through them all.

However far we may wander,

However high we may soar,

All flyers one day turn homeward,

Homeward and earthward once more.

Down through the good air that holds us,

Flying like birds to the nest,

Let the warm darkness enfold us.

Fly to the earth, and then rest.

I leave you the world as I knew it,

The land and the sea, in your care,

Seen from the sky, where I flew it,

I leave you the view from the air.

For A. M. L. and C. A. L.,

who shared a poet's vision and a pilot's view

— R. L. and R. B.

VIKING
Published by the Penguin Group
Penguin Books USA Inc.,
375 Hudson Street, New York, New York 10014, U.S.A.
Penguin Books Ltd, 27 Wrights Lane, London W8 5TZ, England
Penguin Books Australia Ltd, Ringwood, Victoria, Australia
Penguin Books Canada Ltd, 10 Alcorn Avenue, Toronto, Ontario, Canada M4V 3B2
Penguin Books (N.Z.) Ltd, 182–190 Wairau Road, Auckland 10, New Zealand

Penguin Books Ltd, Registered Offices: Harmondsworth, Middlesex, England

First published in 1992 by Viking Penguin, a division of Penguin Books USA Inc.

1   3   5   7   9   10   8   6   4   2

Text copyright © Reeve Lindbergh, 1992
Photographs copyright © Richard Brown, 1992
Library of Congress Cataloging-in-Publication Data
Lindbergh, Reeve.
A view from the air / by Reeve Lindbergh;
illustrated by Richard Brown.   p.   cm.
Summary: The pilot's perspective provides an
enlightening view of man's impact on the earth.
I S B N 0 - 6 7 0 - 8 4 6 6 0 - 0
[1. Flight – Fiction.   2. Airplanes – Fiction.]
I. Brown, Richard, 1945–   ill.   II. Title.
PZ7.L65724Vi 1992 [E] – dc20   92-4062 CIP AC
Printed in U.S.A.
Set in ITC Esprit Medium